Wally Whiner Likes to Whine... WAH! Wah!

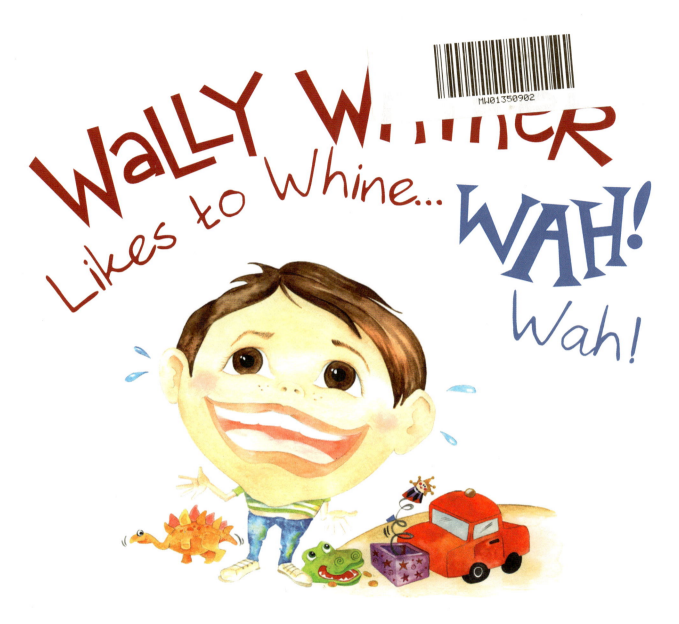

Written by
Deborah Schneider Kraut

And illustrated by
Bonnie LeMaire

Copyright © 2012 Deborah Schneider Kraut

All rights reserved.

ISBN: 1470094886

ISBN 13: 9781470094881

Library of Congress Control Number: 2012903173

CreateSpace Independent Publishing Platform

North Charleston, South Carolina

For my grandson, Shai,
and all our friends and family (little and big),
who have learned the power of words.

My name is Wally Whiner and I really like to whine. Wah! Wah!

My parents say, "Stop it," but I do it all the time. Wah! Wah!

When mom scoots me in the bath,
I whine, "Don't want to go."

I splash and kick and whine so much,
the bathtub overflows.

When dad declares, "It's time for bed,"
I whine, "No! No! Not yet."

I make him chase me 'round the house.
He looks real upset.

Dad shouts, "Use your words, Wally,
and your big boy voice."

But I say, "Whining's much more fun.
That's my big boy choice!"

My name is Wally Whiner
and I really like to whine.

I make a lot of noise,
each and every squealing time.

At school, Ms. Lopez says,
"Use words, you'll be much stronger."

But I ignore Ms. Lopez's advice
and whine even longer.

When Ms. Lopez calls for "Show and Tell,"
I whine, "No! No! Not that!"

Instead of showing Dino off,
I hide him in my hat.

In art class, I whine, "Nooo!" at Ruby, when she asks to use my glue.

"That's not the way to behave," she says. "I don't want to play with you."

I race to my teacher
and whine all the way to her desk.

"Use words instead of whining.
It's a secret to success."

The next day at recess,
I follow Ms. Lopez's advice.

Ruby and I play again.
Hooray! We play so nice.

Ms. Lopez beams, "I'm pleased to say you're doing very well."

"My secret is I stopped whining, as you can surely tell."

At home, I stop my whining
and pick my toys up from the floor.

My parents say, "We're proud of you."
I grin like my dinosaur.

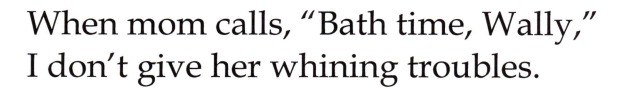

When mom calls, "Bath time, Wally,"
I don't give her whining troubles.

I hop into my soapy bath
and play with all my bubbles.

When dad says, "It's bedtime, Wally,"
I grab my sleeping gear.

I fall asleep right away
and grin from ear to ear.

My name is Wally Whiner,
I USED to really like to whine.

But now I use words, not "Wah! Wah!"
It works every time.

So here's my advice for all the whiners
out there in "reading land."

Be sure to listen carefully
and you'll become a fan.

Use words instead of "Wah! Wah!"
It helps both me and you.

Use words instead of "Wah! Wah!"
That's what big kids do.

THE END

Made in the USA
Charleston, SC
24 January 2013